January 1994
Especially for Jillian,
with the authors
love!

Grandma's Scrapbook

BY JOSEPHINE NOBISSO

ILLUSTRATED BY
MAUREEN HYDE

Green Tiger Press
Published by Simon & Schuster   New York London Toronto   Sydney Tokyo Singapore

ACKNOWLEDGEMENT

The author wishes to gratefully acknowledge Southampton College of Long Island University for its generosity in allowing her the use of The John Steinbeck Room where this book was written.

GREEN TIGER PRESS
Simon & Schuster Building, Rockefeller Center
1230 Avenue of the Americas, New York, New York 10020
Text copyright © 1990 by Josephine Nobisso
Illustrations copyright © 1990 by Maureen Hyde
GREEN TIGER PRESS is a trademark of Simon & Schuster.
Manufactured in Hong Kong

10   9   8   7   6   5   4   3   2

Library of Congress Cataloging-in-Publication Data
Nobisso, Josephine. Grandma's scrapbook / by Josephine Nobisso ;
illustrated by Maureen Hyde.   p.   cm.   Summary: A scrapbook
provides many memories of good times enjoyed with Grandma.
[1. Grandmother — Fiction.   2. Scrapbooks — Fiction.]
I. Hyde, Maureen, ill.   II. Title.   PZ7.N6645Gr   1991
[E] — dc20   91-23309   CIP   ISBN 0-671-74976-5

For my mother Mary (Maria) Zamboli Nobisso who, at the age of 65, stopped a Long Island Railroad train with the power of her devotion and love.

And for her four granddaughters: Nicolle, Gina, Bianca and Kali, all middle-named Marie in honor of the two great mothers of the world.

—J.N.

To Mary and Eliese, with special thanks to Ali, Shana and Louise

—M.H.

*G*randma's hair was once black as crows. I was too young to remember, but I know it was so because Grandma kept a scrapbook.

*T*he first pages are of me as a baby — looking dopey before I fall asleep, and silly as I yawn, and like a monkey with ears so big, and coconut-head so bald. Here's a tiny envelope with wisps of baby hair in it. And beside it, a braided lock of Grandma's hair, black as crows.

*H*ere I am in my stroller, Grandma laughing as she pushes me through the garden. See that mashed flower in my fist? I used to grab them as we passed, until Grandma managed to teach me to snip them just right.

Here's that first flower, faded, pressed between the pages of the scrapbook.

I'm older in these. Just looking brings back the smell of salt air in her back yard, and of crushed grass, and of fishy bay mud on Bella's paws. I can hear the frogs and the crickets, and the water lapping against the sea wall.

From the dock we watched red evenings turn to black nights. Then Grandma would call every star she knew by name. The next thing I knew, it was morning, and I was under a quilt in my room at Grandma's. She'd carry me in all by herself.

In the scrapbook she saved a seashell I'd once clasped in my hand.

Here we are another year, in bathing suits and hats — me all arms and legs, and Grandma a natural beauty. We were having cocoa in fancy chipped cups, being proper and elegant and giggly.

*S*he rode me on the back of her bicycle, and in the village we bought a picnic lunch.

"How far to the ocean?" I asked.

"Half a mile as the crow flies," Grandma told me. She peddled to the edge of a field, and we watched the bright blue skies. A seagull flapped by. Grandma shrugged and laughed her wonderful laugh. "It's not a crow, but it'll know the way!" She followed it, swerving to avoid the gopher holes. Then the bird turned and flew the other way.

"Hey!" Grandma called, laughing and shaking her fist at the sky. "Where are you taking us?"

But already I could hear the waves, roaring as they broke and sighing as they slid back into the sea. And already I could see the bridge. "That way! That way, Grandma!" I cried.

At each wave, Grandma lifted me over her head, taking a dunking herself. She sputtered as she came up, and I squealed the next warning: "A wave! A wave!", so that she could bob and dance with the ocean's rolls. "A wave!" I called to the gulls.

*S*he took me shopping. I picked funny face mugs for my parents, a "Maw" and a "Paw". There was a reflecting heart for Bella's collar, and a sparkling ring bigger than an acorn for Grandma.

That was the year she bought me the camera. We took nutty shots of each other, and this one of Bella wearing my sunglasses. Then we rode the dirt paths home through the woods, breaking their silence with our cackling.

When it cooled in the evenings, she taught me about picking garden greens for dinner and flowers for the table. Sometimes Grandma's friends came, and we all howled songs around the piano. She'd send everyone home early — "Because there's a child in the house!" And sometimes she'd take out the scrapbook. "What times we've had!" I told her.

"Yes," she agreed, "every year we change and grow." And the scrapbook was making everything more precious, as though without it, some of the memories would be lost.

At night Grandma read to me from my favorite books on her shelves. Sometimes I fell asleep dreaming about the rolling, rushing sea. A wave! A wave!

My parents didn't come to pick me up one year. "You're big enough to ride the train alone," Grandma told me.

The sting from my sun-burned cheeks worked itself into my eyes. "See you next year, Grandma!" I told her through my tears. "And it'll be even better!"

"Every year is better!" she whispered into my hair, black as crows, like hers used to be. Through the train window, I took this picture of Grandma on the platform, waving, her acorn-diamond ring sparkling a good-bye.

Every year was better for years and years.

And last year, when I woke up at Grandma's house, I took her for a stroll in her wheelchair. I walked her through the paths in the woods, and around the gopher holes in the field. I brought her to the water's edge so that she could feel the pulse of waves on her feet. We rode between the garden rows, picking the greens we needed, and overflowing her lap with firm, fresh flowers.

And even though I collected for the scrapbook all summer long, there were still a lot of blank pages left when she died.

Grandma started that scrapbook because I was once too young to remember, and because one day, I may get too old to remember. My Grandma's gone this year, but somehow she remains, keeping me from forgetting. And sometimes, when I'm all by myself and dreaming of the sea, I can almost feel her right here beside me, filling in the blank pages of my life, her sparkling ring glinting off my hair, black as crows. Like hers used to be.